Max's Dragon

KATE BANKS   Pictures by BORIS KULIKOV

FRANCES FOSTER BOOKS ❧ FARRAR, STRAUS AND GIROUX ❧ NEW YORK

Text copyright © 2008 by Kate Banks
Pictures copyright © 2008 by Boris Kulikov
Distributed in Canada by Douglas & McIntyre Ltd.
Color separations by Chroma Graphics PTE Ltd.
Printed and bound in the United States of America by Phoenix Color Corporation
Designed by Robbin Gourley
First edition, 2008
10 9 8 7 6 5 4 3 2 1

www.fsgkidsbooks.com

Library of Congress Cataloging-in-Publication Data
Banks, Kate, date.
    Max's Dragon / Kate Banks ; pictures by Boris Kulikov.— 1st ed.
        p.   cm.
    Summary: Many unusual and unexpected things happen while Max plays with
his invisible dragon.
    ISBN-13: 978-0-374-39921-4
    ISBN-10: 0-374-39921-2
    [1. Dragons—Fiction.   2. Imagination—Fiction.   3. Imaginary playmates—
Fiction.   4. Play—Fiction.]   I. Kulikov, Boris, ill.   II. Title.

PZ7.B22594 Mau 2008
[E]—dc22   2007060727

For Peter, Max's brother — K.B.

To Larisa and Peter Konnikov — B.K.

Max skipped across the lawn.

His brothers, Karl and Benjamin, were playing croquet.

"Found, ground," said Max.

"What are you doing?" Karl asked.

"I'm looking for words that rhyme," said Max.

"Look what I found on the ground."

Max picked up an umbrella.

"Who needs that," said Ben. "It's not raining."

Max opened the umbrella and ducked underneath.

"Ready?" he said.

"Who are you talking to?" asked Ben.

"My dragon," said Max.

"Dragons don't exist," said Karl.

"Yes they do," said Max.

"There's a dragon in my wagon."

Karl looked into the wagon.

"We're playing hide-and-seek," said Max.

"So please don't peek."

"Sorry," said Karl.

He and Ben began to laugh.

Ben hit his ball through a wicket.
It rolled across the lawn.
Max raced off.
"Where are you going?" said Karl.
"My dragon's tail has made a trail," said Max.
"I'm following it."

Then Max lay down in the grass and looked up at the clouds.

Karl put down his mallet.

"What are you doing now?" he asked.

"My dragon's trying to practice flying," said Max.

"I still don't see him," said Ben.

"He's up there, dancing on air," said Max.

"I still say there's no such thing as a dragon," said Karl.

Then along came a big black cloud.

"Uh-oh," said Max. "Oh, no."

"Hey, that cloud looks like a dinosaur," said Ben.

"It's going after your dragon!" said Karl.

"If my dragon isn't faster, there'll be a big disaster," said Max.

"The dinosaur is getting closer," said Ben.

The wind began to whistle.

It blew the hat off Karl's head.

It whispered in Ben's ears.

Max zipped up his sweatshirt.

"My dragon's sneeze makes quite a breeze," he said.

The sky turned purple.
Thunder rumbled and clapped.
Karl and Ben jumped.
"My dragon's fury makes me worry," said Max.

The rain began.

Max put up his umbrella.

Karl and Ben were shivering.

"My dragon's roar has made it pour," said Max.

"What can we do to stop it?" cried Karl.

"Get rid of the dinosaur," said Max.

"How?" said Ben.

"You need to make a rhyme," said Max.

"The dinosaur fell into the well," said Karl.

"Where he had to stay for the rest of the day," said Ben.

Suddenly the rain dwindled to a drizzle.

The thunder ceased.

The wind died down.

The clouds parted.

And out came the sun.

"It worked!" said Ben.

"Where's your dragon now?" asked Karl.

"My dragon thought it best to take a little rest," said Max.

Karl and Ben went back to playing croquet.

"Where's my ball?" said Ben.

Max poked his umbrella into the bushes.

"I see something round lying on the ground," he said.

"Is it another dragon?" said Ben.

"No," said Max, leaning over. "It's a croquet ball."

Max handed it to Ben.
"Thanks," said Ben.

"Would you like to play croquet?" Karl said to Max.
"I don't know how, but I'd like to learn," said Max.
"Then take a turn," said Karl.
And he handed Max a mallet.

Max hit the ball with the mallet.

It bounded across the grass and out of sight.

"Where did it go?" asked Karl.

"It rolled over the clover," said Max.

"And through a wicket and into a thicket," said Ben.

There was a rumbling in the distance.

"What's that?" asked Karl.

"It's my dragon," said Max.

"What's he doing now?" said Ben.

"He's snoring," said Max.

Suddenly the rain began again.

"We need to make a rhyme!" said Karl.

Max popped open his umbrella.

"Don't be upset about getting wet," he said.

"Because, as you can see, there's room for three."